Sports Illustrated KIDS

I Don't Want to Live on the Tennis Court

by Val Priebe

illustrated by Jorge Santillan

STONE ARCH BOOKS
a capstone imprint

VICTORY SCHOOL SUPERSTARS

Sports Illustrated KIDS *I Don't Want to Live on the Tennis Court*
is published by Stone Arch Books — A Capstone Imprint
1710 Roe Crest Drive
North Mankato, Minnesota 56003
www.capstonepub.com

Art Director: Bob Lentz
Graphic Designer: Hilary Wacholz
Production Specialist: Michelle Biedscheid

Timeline photo credits: Library of Congress (top right); Sports
Illustrated/Bob Martin (middle right & bottom left); Manny
Millan (top left); Simon Bruty (bottom right).

Printed in the United States of America in Stevens Point,
Wisconsin.
102011
006404WZS12

Library of Congress Cataloging-in-Publication Data
Priebe, Val.
  I don't want to live on the tennis court / by Val Priebe; illustrated by
Jorge H. Santillan.
     p. cm. — (Sports illustrated kids. Victory School superstars)
  Summary: Carmen's new friend Laura is super at tennis, but she is also
tired of it and would like to try other sports—can Carmen convince Laura
to talk to her mother about her frustration?
  ISBN 978-1-4342-3761-3 (library binding)
  ISBN 978-1-4342-3868-9 (pbk.)
  1. Tennis stories. 2. Friendship—Juvenile fiction. [1. Tennis—Fiction.
2. Friendship—Fiction.] I. Santillan, Jorge, ill. II. Title. III. Title: I do not
want to live on the tennis court. IV. Series: Sports Illustrated kids. Victory
School superstars.

PZ7.P934287Iah 2012
813.6—dc23   2011033773

TABLE of CONTENTS

CARMEN SKORE

Tennis

AGE: 10
GRADE: 4
SUPER SPORTS ABILITY: Super Dribbling

VICTORY SCHOOL SUPERSTARS

ALICIA

DANNY

KENZIE

TYLER

JOSH

VICTORY SCHOOL MAP

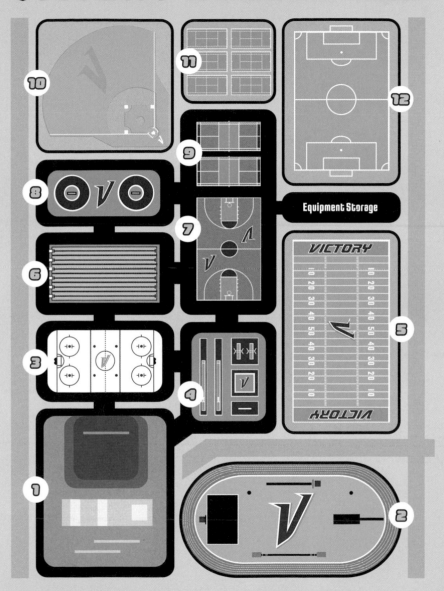

1. BMX/Skateboarding
2. Track and Field
3. Hockey/Figure Skating
4. Gymnastics
5. Football
6. Swimming
7. Basketball
8. Wrestling
9. Volleyball
10. Baseball/Softball
11. Tennis
12. Soccer

Equipment Storage

Tennis Time

Bounce . . . bounce . . . bounce . . .

Even though we're playing tennis in gym this week, I can't help but dribble the ball!

I play basketball at Victory Sports School. Victory is a special school for athletes with super skills. My super skill is dribbling. Nobody can steal the basketball from me!

"Carmen, that's not a basketball!" says Lynsey, my best friend. I finish dribbling the tennis ball between my legs and grin at her.

From the corner of my eye, I see a girl looking at me and smiling. I think her name is Laura. Her super skill is in tennis.

"Quiet down, class!" says our gym teacher, Coach Brad. "Time for your first tennis lesson."

"Well, the first tennis lesson for most of you," he says, smiling. He points to Laura. "For those of you who don't know, Laura is Victory's best tennis player."

Laura's face turns red all the way to her ears. Normally, everyone at Victory is proud of their super skill, but she seems embarrassed.

Coach Brad hands me a tennis racquet and interrupts my thoughts. He shows us how to serve, and then tells us to partner up. The only person that can be Laura's partner is Coach Brad. I stop serving to watch.

WHAM!

Coach serves the ball as hard as he can. His face is red afterward. Laura's face doesn't change. She hits the ball back to Coach, who barely taps it back. Laura watches the ball, winds up, and . . . *SLAM!*

She pounds the ball as far from
Coach Brad as she can without the ball
going out-of-bounds. Coach Brad watches
the ball fly away from him.

He smiles and shakes his head. "Good
return, Laura. Class dismissed!" he says.

Later, after school, Laura and I are walking out of the building at the same time. It's my chance to talk to her.

"Hey, Laura!" I say. "You were so great in gym class today."

"Thanks," Laura says quietly. "I thought your dribbling was great."

"Thanks!" I say. "It *is* my super skill. I just can't help it!"

"When did you know dribbling was your super skill?" Laura asks, laughing.

"I was six," I reply. "What about you?"

Suddenly, a horn starts honking in the parking lot. We both look up. Laura doesn't answer.

"Gotta go!" Laura says. "Tennis lessons."

"See you tomorrow!" I call to Laura. I can't help but think, Laura's the best. Why does she need lessons?

CHAPTER 2

A Real Match

"Hey, do you want to go to the tennis match?" Lynsey asks me after school the next day.

"Sure! I'd love to see Laura play for real," I say.

We head straight to the tennis courts behind the school. The bleachers are full. Laura is warming up her arms by swinging her racquet. Then she stretches out her legs. She looks determined.

The other girl serves to start the match. *BLAM!* She hits the ball toward Laura.

Just like in gym class, Laura easily returns the ball over the net. The other tennis player is fast and hits the ball back to Laura.

Without even moving, Laura hits the ball back in the other direction. The other player hits the ball back right to where Laura is standing.

Instead of hitting the ball as hard as she can, Laura gives it a small tap with her racquet. It barely goes over the net. The other player is on the other side of the court. She runs as fast as she can.

Bounce . . . bounce. The ball hits the ground two times before she can reach it. Laura scores another point!

"That was really smart!" Lynsey says to me. I nod in agreement.

Laura's strategy reminds me of really good passers in basketball. They make their defenders think they're passing one way, and then they go the other way.

We cheer as loud as we can. I see her look up in the stands at us. She looks happy to see us.

After the tennis match is over, Laura finds us.

"Thanks for coming," she says. "It was nice to have fans cheering for me!"

"Great returns, Laura!" I tell her. "You'd be a really good passer on the basketball floor."

"Laura!" a woman's voice calls. "Time to go!"

Laura's face is suddenly sad. Then she looks up and calls, "Coming, Mom!" She turns to us and says, "I gotta go. Mom probably wants to talk about the match. My serve was awful."

"But you won," I say.

Laura just shrugs, slumps her shoulders, and walks away.

CHAPTER 3

Laura's Story

The next day, I see Laura in the gym on the way to lunch. She is not practicing her serve like I thought she would be. She is dribbling the tennis ball like I did.

"Trying out for basketball?" I ask with a smile.

Laura jumps. The ball hits her foot.

"I was just goofing around," Laura says. Her face is red again. "What's up?"

"I wanted to tell you again how great you were yesterday," I say.

"Thanks, Carmen," says Laura. "It was nice of you to come. I should probably work on my serve, though." Laura turns to get her ball.

"Why are you so worried about your serve?" asks Lynsey, coming up behind me. "It's perfect!"

"I've never been good at serving. Not like —" Laura stops, "not as good as I should be if I'm going to make the national team."

"Nationals? Wow!" I say.

"Only if my serve gets better," says Laura. She sees we are confused. "It's a long story," she says. "Let's go to lunch. I'll tell you there."

At the lunchroom, we get our food and sit down to talk. Laura starts to tell her story.

"When I was three, my parents gave me a tennis racquet for my birthday," she says. "They were hoping I had a super skill, even though I was really young."

Laura takes a break and sighs. "My mom and I practiced every day until I was too tired to move," she continues. "But one day, not even my mom could get a ball past me. I was five years old. After that, my mom signed me up for every club she could find. I have a private coach, too. Now I only practice against adults."

"Wow! Those are some serious skills," says Lynsey.

"They were really excited," Laura continues. "My mom played tennis. Her serve is the best! She went to nationals. Anyway, I have always played tennis, even when I wanted to do — um, other stuff."

"Like soccer?" asks Lynsey. She thinks everyone should play soccer.

"Soccer and lots of other things," says Laura. "But everything gets in the way of tennis." Laura looks sad. "I don't want to live on the tennis court anymore!"

Basketball Basics?

That night at home, I couldn't stop thinking about Laura's problem. I decided to talk it over with my dad.

"Dad, remember when I asked you if I could play soccer?" I ask.

"Yes," says Dad. "Do you want to play something else now?"

"No," I say, "but what did you think when I asked?"

"I worried that you didn't want to play basketball anymore," says Dad. "Basketball is my favorite. But I knew it was important to try new things."

That's what I thought he would say!

"Thanks, Dad!" I say, giving him a hug. I can't wait to talk to Laura tomorrow.

The next day at school, I hurry to put my backpack away. Then I start looking for Laura, but I don't have to look long. She is walking right toward me.

"LAURA!" I shout. Laura is so surprised she drops her books on the floor.

"Sorry!" I say. I help pick up her books. I notice one called *Basketball Basics*. Laura snaps the book up before I can look closer.

"Laura, what is it?" I ask. "We're friends. You can tell me!"

"You saw the basketball book, right?" she asks.

Suddenly, everything made sense — the way Laura looked at me in gym, dribbling her tennis ball, and the basketball book.

"Do you want to play basketball?" I ask.

"I really want to play a team sport," Laura says. "I want to play *with* other kids, not just against them! All I do is go to school and play tennis. I don't have many friends or any brothers or sisters." Laura looks down. "I'm lonely."

"You should just try out then. Don't be nervous," I say.

"It's not that I'm nervous," Laura says. "I don't think my mom will let me. I have always played tennis, and my mom only played tennis. It's her favorite sport."

"My dad *loves* basketball," I tell her.
"I was nervous about asking him to play
soccer. But he said yes! Trying new things
is good. It might even make you better at
tennis," I say. "Ask her!"

"I guess it couldn't hurt," Laura says.

Future Teammates

The next day after school, I race to find Laura and wish her luck before her tennis match. For the first time since we became friends, I see her really smile.

"Carmen, I asked my mom about basketball. And guess what?" Laura says. "She said yes!"

"That's great, Laura. I knew it would work," I say, giving her a big hug.

"Thank you SO much. I never could have talked to my mom without you!" Laura says. "Now I just have to win this tennis match today."

"You'll be great!" I say.

"I hope so," says Laura. "If I win today, I will probably make the national team."

As the match begins, Laura finally looks happy to be playing her super sport. It will probably help her game, too. I know I always play better when I'm happy!

BAM! Laura serves first. I can tell that she's happy with her serve. She already has the other tennis player running around the court while she waits for a return.

The other player doesn't even get a turn to serve, and at least half of Laura's serves are aces! When the other player *does* return a serve, Laura never lets a ball go by her. She wins the first set very fast.

The second set doesn't go as well. The other player is a good server. Laura has a hard time returning her serves, despite her super skill. She loses the second set by one point.

The tie-breaking set seems to go on forever. Laura serves first, but the other player seems determined not to lose.

WHAM! She returns Laura's serve, but Laura is ready. She hits the ball right at the other player. After a few more hits, Laura returns with a hit so hard, the ball gets stuck in the fence after the bounce. The girl was expecting Laura's soft return. It's match point!

Laura winds up and serves. The other girl returns. The players hit back and forth. Laura finishes the match with a drop shot. This one hits the top of the net, nearly stops, and then falls onto the opponent's side of the court. Laura wins!

"What a shot!" I say, running up to Laura after the game.

"Slam dunk," replies Laura. She gives me a knowing wink. "Looks like basketball is already making me a better tennis player. I owe it all to you."

I just grin and ask, "What are future teammates for?"

GLOSSARY

aces (AYSS-es)—serves in tennis that are not returned or even touched by the other player

determined (di-TUR-mind)—not weak or uncertain

dismissed (diss-MISSD)—allowed to leave

dribble (DRIB-uhl)—bounce a ball over and over, keeping it under control

embarrassed (em-BA-ruhssd)—feeling awkward or uncomfortable

interrupts (in-tuh-RUHPTS)—stops or hinders something for a short time

match point (MACH POYNT)—the point that wins the match

national team (NASH-uh-nuhl TEEM)—a sports team made of the best players in a country

serve (SURV)—to send the ball to the other player to begin play

strategy (STRAT-uh-jee)—a clever plan for winning

ABOUT THE AUTHOR

VAL PRIEBE

Val Priebe lives in St. Paul, Minnesota, with her four dogs, a cat named Cowboy, and a guy named Nick. When she's not writing, she enjoys coaching basketball, running, knitting, and trying out new recipes. Val is also the author of *It's Hard to Dribble with Your Feet* and *Five Fouls and You're Out,* and *I Only Surf Online* from the Victory School Superstars series.

ABOUT THE ILLUSTRATOR

JORGE SANTILLAN

Jorge Santillan got his start illustrating in the children's sections of local newspapers. He opened his own illustration studio in 2005. His creative team specializes in books, comics, and children's magazines. Jorge lives in Mendoza, Argentina, with his wife, Bety; son, Luca; and their four dogs, Fito, Caro, Angie, and Sammy.

TENNIS IN HISTORY

1873   A new game *sphairistikè* is played on an hour-glass shaped court. It becomes known as tennis.

1875   The tennis court is changed to a rectangular court, measuring the same as today's courts.

1877   The first World Tennis Championship is held in Wimbledon in England.

1920   France's Suzanne Lenglen is the first player to win the triple crown of ladies singles, ladies doubles, and mixed doubles.

1949   American Gussy Moran shocks Wimbledon with her tennis dress and lace-trimmed knickers. She is on the front pages of newspapers worldwide.

1980   Tennis is played at Wimbledon on Sunday for the first time.

1990   Martina Navratilova wins Wimbledon for a record ninth time.

2002   Sisters Venus and Serena Williams are ranked numbers one and two in the world.

2006   Andre Agassi, one of the most popular players of all time, retires.

2011   At the U.S. Open, Swiss player Roger Federer advances to a record thirtieth quarterfinal match.

Carmen Skore Can't Be Stopped!

If you liked reading Carmen's tennis adventure, check out her other sports stories.

Five Fouls and You're Out!

When it comes to dribbling, Carmen shines on the basketball court. But on defense, she keeps racking up fouls. If she doesn't stop fouling, every game will end the same — five fouls and she's out!

I Only Surf Online

Carmen is learning to surf on a school trip. While her new friend Sarah is surfing like a pro, Carmen keeps wiping out. Will a mystery surfer inspire Carmen and help her ride the waves, or will Carmen only surf online?

It's Hard to Dribble with Your Feet

Carmen is a star basketball dribbler. But when she plays soccer, handling the ball isn't as easy. Now girls are talking about her, and she feels awful. She just didn't know that it's hard to dribble with your feet.

VICT

SCH

SUPE